The AMAZING DAYS of ABBY HAYES®

It's Music to My Ears

ANNE MAZER

AN
APPLE
PAPERBACK

SCHOLASTIC INC.
New York Toronto London Auckland Sydney
Mexico City New Delhi Hong Kong Buenos Aires

ISBN 0-439-68063-8

Text copyright © 2004 by Anne Mazer.
All rights reserved. Published by Scholastic Inc.

SCHOLASTIC, APPLE PAPERBACKS, THE AMAZING DAYS OF ABBY HAYES, and associated logos are trademarks and/or registered trademarks of Scholastic Inc.

12 11 10 9 8 7 6 5 4   5 6 7 8 9 10/0

Printed in the U.S.A.

First printing, January 2005

Chapter 1

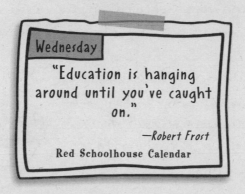

After a few months of hanging around Susan B. Anthony Middle School, I think I'm finally catching on to sixth grade! Hooray!

Today we start a new cycle. Most of my classes stay the same. But instead of health class, I have art.

Three Reasons I Didn't Like Health Class:

1. I got off to a bad start. On the very first day, I ran, slipped, and had a spectacular fall in front of EVERYONE.

2. No one ever forgot. Especially Victoria, one of the meanest girls in the sixth grade, who teased me about it for a long time.

3. Health class was boring. We studied things like healthy eating habits, food groups, balanced meals, and nutrition. Learning to eat is like learning to breathe. <u>DUH!</u>

<u>Four Reasons I Hope Art Class Will Be Better:</u>

1. I plan to walk **slowly** into the class-room on the first day.

2. The art teacher won't compare me to Eva and Isabel, my brilliant twin sisters. She doesn't know them. It's her first year of teaching middle school. (Hooray!)

3. My friend Natalie had art last cycle and said it was great. She liked the teacher, too.

4. Painting, sculpting, and drawing are fun!

Five Reasons I'm Beginning to Like Middle School:

1. I know the routine.
2. I like most of my teachers.
3. I've made new friends.
4. Victoria stopped teasing me.
5. The library is HUGE!

Six Reasons I Will Quit Writing These Lists Now:

1. They're getting too long!
2. I can't think of any more answers.
3. I can't think of any more questions.
4. Don't I have something better to do?
5. Like, my homework.
6. I better stop now or else. . . .

GOOD-BYE!!!!!

In the gym locker room, Abby kicked off her sneakers and tossed them into her locker. They clanged against the metal wall.

On the other side of the locker room, Natalie jumped at the noise. "You don't have to throw them!" she cried.

What's the big deal? Abby thought. The locker room was noisy. Girls called to one another, banged doors open and shut, and ran the water in the sinks.

Abby apologized, anyway. "Sorry," she said to Natalie. "I didn't mean to startle you." She took her shoes and regular clothes from her locker, then sat down on the wooden bench to change.

"Wasn't that fun?" Abby's best friend, Hannah, slid onto the bench next to her. She was wearing a bright orange sweatshirt and sweatpants.

Orange was one of Hannah's favorite colors. She had a lot of others, too. Abby remembered her saying that she loved every color in the rainbow. Hannah was enthusiastic about *everything*.

"Don't you love gym class?" Hannah cried.

"Not the warm-ups," Abby said. "Especially not the sit-ups and push-ups."

"They're not as much fun as volleyball or soccer," Hannah admitted. She took a hairbrush out of her backpack and began to brush her hair vigorously. "But I like jogging."

"I collapsed after only a few laps," Abby confessed. She made a muscle with her right arm and frowned at it. "I'm just a puny eighty-nine-pound weakling."

"No, you're not!" Hannah put down her brush and circled her long hair with a ponytail holder. She was not only enthusiastic, she was encouraging, too. Hannah loved to cheer on her friends.

"Thanks," Abby said, although she wasn't convinced. It would take more than friendly words to make her believe that she was a good runner.

She glanced at her curly red hair in the mirror and sighed. Even now that she had it cut shorter, it was still wild and unruly.

"Did you see Mason jogging?" Hannah asked. "He's faster than anyone in our class. I can't believe it."

In elementary school, Mason had never been an athlete. He had been known for his practical jokes and loud laugh. His nickname in fifth grade had been "the Big Burper." Over the summer he had shot up and slimmed down. He had also speeded up.

"If you think Mason's changed," Abby said in a low voice, "what about some of our other classmates? Like *her*?" She pointed at a girl primping in front of a mirror.

It was Crystal. She had been in the other fifth-grade class at Lancaster Elementary. Last year she had been an annoying but normal elementary school student. Now as Abby and Hannah watched, she applied lipstick, eyeliner, and blush with a practiced hand. Her skirt was short and tight; she wore lace-up boots and a skimpy sweater.

"She's changed big-time," Hannah agreed.

Abby brushed some lint from her pants. "Why do girls do all that stuff to make boys notice them?" she asked. "*I'd* never do it!"

"Me, neither," Natalie said, joining them. She ran her hands through her short dark hair.

Hannah sighed. "I don't get it. I mean, boys are fine, but why do girls have to change their personalities for them?"

"It's always a mistake to try too hard," Natalie pronounced. She leaned against a locker and stared into the distance.

"How come your socks always match now?" Abby asked Natalie. "I miss seeing green stripes on your left foot and gray polka dots on your right."

"I used to check out your socks first thing every day," Hannah added. "It was like the daily sock watch."

Natalie shrugged and didn't answer.

Abby stared at her. Maybe Natalie wasn't boy-crazy, but she was still *so* different from the old Natalie. She wasn't the girl who did chemistry experiments in her room and acted out scenes from fantasy novels. She wasn't the girl who wore paint-splattered sneakers anymore.

Something essential had changed in her personality. Since she had arrived in middle school, Natalie was ultracool. She knew about bands that no one else had ever heard of. Her hair and clothes were big-city and so was her attitude.

Abby hardly knew how to act around her anymore.

Now Natalie picked up her backpack and clarinet case. "I've got to go," she said. "I have an audition for the new jazz band. Have you heard about it?"

Abby shook her head.

"The director is a famous trombonist. He performs all over the U.S. and Europe." Natalie sounded excited, almost like her old self. "He's going to select the best musicians in the school for the jazz band. Rehearsals are starting right away. Only a few kids are going to make it. I hope I'm one of them."

"Good luck!" Hannah said.

"Break a leg," Abby chimed in. "Oops — that's for the theater, isn't it?"

"Whatever," Natalie said. She hurried out of the locker room. The door swung shut behind her.

"What's happened to her?" Abby wailed. "I miss the old Natalie!"

"She's grown up, I guess," Hannah said with a shrug. "It's supposed to happen to all of us."

"Not me," Abby said. "I'll never change who I am." She slammed her locker door shut and turned the combination lock.

"What about your new haircut?" Hannah asked. "And your new clothes?"

"That's all outside," Abby said. "I won't change *inside*. My personality and feelings are still the same as they've always been."

She glanced at her image in the mirror again. *"This* is my biggest change in sixth grade!" Abby pointed to her earlobes. "I did it for me, not for anyone else."

"I still can't believe you went through with it," Hannah said.

In the first week of sixth grade, Abby had gotten her ears pierced secretly. When she had unveiled her earrings in front of the entire Hayes family, her parents had been angry and shocked. But Abby didn't regret anything, even the hours of community service her mother had decided to make her do.

It had been worth it. Every time Abby looked in the mirror and caught the gleam of an earring, she felt a thrill of happiness.

She had made a decision, followed through with it, and accepted the consequences. Her pierced ears reminded her daily of her own strength. And Abby needed that daily reminder. . . .

"Where's your next class?" Hannah said.

"Upstairs." Abby picked up her backpack. "I've got to run."

The two friends said good-bye. Abby hurried toward the door.

She turned one last time to wave at Hannah and then plunged into the crowd of middle-school students.

"Careful!" someone said.

Abby looked up. A boy stood directly in front of her. His hand gripped her shoulder.

"You almost crashed into me," he said, smiling.

"I did?" She hadn't even seen him. But that wasn't unusual in the insane rush-hour-style middle-school hallways.

The boy nodded at her. He was tall, with brown hair. He wore a zippered blue fleece sweater and jeans. He was smiling. His eyes had a friendly expression.

In one hand, he held an instrument case.

His other hand was still holding her at arm's length.

"You can let go of my shoulder now," Abby said.

"Am I safe?" he joked.

"For now," Abby retorted.

Their eyes met. Or maybe they had been staring at each other for a while. Was he staring at her? Was *she* staring at *him*?

Abby suddenly felt numb. She couldn't speak. Her mouth went dry. Her head felt like a hot-air balloon. Her face began to burn.

She turned and bolted down the hall.

Chapter 2

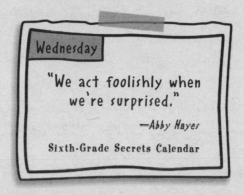

The Surprise:

1. I was surprised when I almost ran into a strange boy.

2. I was surprised when he grabbed my shoulder to stop me.

3. I was surprised when I looked at him.

4. I was surprised by what his eyes looked like.

The Foolishness:

1. WHY did I stare at him?

2. What did he think?

3. My face was all red.

4. Did he notice how embarrassed I was?

5. Why did I run away like that?

More Surprising Foolishness:

1. I can't stop thinking about him.

2. Who is he, anyway?

3. Is he a sixth-grader? Or a seventh- or an eighth-grader?

4. Will I "run into" him again?

5. I hope not!

6. I NEVER want to see him again.

That's not true. I've lied to my journal! I'm <u>dying</u> to see him again. I want to know his name, his favorite subject, and what he does after school. Does he live near me? I wish we had some classes together. I can't wait until school tomorrow.

And I can't believe I'm writing this.

Abby slid her lunch tray onto the almost empty table facing the windows.

It was lunch period on Thursday. There was one

other person sitting at the table. She sat with her back to the noisy cafeteria, one arm protectively circling an open sketchbook.

"Hi," Abby said.

Sophia looked up, startled. They ate lunch together almost every day now, but she always seemed surprised to see Abby show up at her table.

"Hi," she said shyly. Sophia's hair was long, dark, and wavy. She wore a turquoise shirt and dark jeans over scuffed leather boots.

"What are you drawing today?" Abby asked.

Sophia pushed the notebook across the table to Abby. There were pages and pages of sketches. Sunflowers cascaded down the sides, odd faces peered from every corner, cats crept along margins, and a row of high-heeled shoes marched diagonally across an empty page.

"I wish I could draw like you." Abby sighed.

"They're just doodles," Sophia protested.

"No, they're *really* good."

Sophia ducked her head, embarrassed.

"You have to illustrate one of my stories." Abby had been keeping a journal for over a year now. She also had a collection of poems, essays, and stories hidden in her desk.

"If you think my drawings are good enough . . ."

"They're great!" Abby cried.

"Mmm-hmm." Sophia took back her notebook, flipped to a fresh page, and began to doodle furiously.

With only a brief glance at her subject, Sophia was able to capture a moment perfectly. Abby watched as girls and boys, caught in the act of eating lunch, began to appear on the page.

One girl shoveled a spoonful of mashed potatoes into her mouth. A boy was throwing a noodle. Another girl blew bubbles in her milk carton.

"They're hilarious!" Abby exclaimed. "You ought to publish them in the school newspaper!"

Sophia stopped, her pen poised above the page. To Abby's surprise, she nodded. "Maybe," she said. Then she clammed up again.

Sophia was the shyest person Abby had ever known. It had taken weeks before Sophia had said anything beyond "hi" and "bye." But now she and Abby spoke every day. It was true that Abby did most of the talking. But she didn't mind.

Abby loved having an artist friend. The two girls sometimes discussed doing a project together. There were lots of possibilities. Sophia might illustrate one of her stories. Or they might collaborate on a picture book. Or they might write a comic strip about middle school. . . .

"Today we have our first art class," Abby said. She and Sophia had many of the same classes. "I can't wait!"

Sophia didn't answer. She picked at her lunch.

"I heard the new art teacher is really good," Abby continued. "Natalie said it was one of her best classes last cycle."

"Natalie?" Sophia knew who she was, but never spoke to her. When she saw Abby's other friends, she disappeared. She was too shy. She even seemed scared of Hannah, the friendliest person in the sixth grade.

"And Natalie has high standards," Abby said. Too high, she thought. Especially since she had entered middle school.

"Oh," Sophia said.

Abby smiled. "The teacher's name is Ms. Bean. Isn't that the greatest name? She could name her kids String or Lima."

Sophia's eyes lit up. She sketched a row of green beans in her notebook, hanging over the kids like vines.

"I hope Ms. Bean is as creative as everyone says," Sophia said after a moment. "I had an art teacher in elementary school who made everyone draw the exact same things in the exact same way. You couldn't even choose your own colors."

"That must have been awful!" Abby said. "If I had a writing teacher like that, I'd hate it!"

"Lucky you didn't," Sophia said. She had heard all about Ms. Bunder, Abby's fifth-grade creative writing teacher.

"Ms. Bunder was the *best*!" Abby cried. "Her assignments were so much fun! She always encouraged me to try new things."

"I had a good teacher at the art museum," Sophia said. "I took classes there on Saturday mornings. But in school, the teacher never liked anything I did."

"She didn't like your artwork?" Abby said in astonishment. "Impossible!"

Sophia glanced at Abby, then looked away.

Abby didn't press her for more information. If she asked too many questions, Sophia would stop talking. Maybe in a day or two, Abby would find out why Sophia's art teacher didn't like her drawings.

Abby picked up a fork. She had almost forgotten

about her lunch. And there were only ten minutes left before the bell rang.

"I want to ask you something," Sophia said.

"What?" Abby took a bite of baked lasagna. It tasted like last year's leftovers.

"It's funny that you mentioned the school newspaper," she said slowly. "They need artists."

"*Yes!*" Abby cried. "You should do it!"

Sophia turned red. "Do you think . . . ?"

"I do. You're a fantastic artist. The newspaper will *love* you. . . ." She was about to say more, but a group of kids entered the cafeteria and caught her eye.

They were laughing and talking. Natalie was at the center, surrounded by a bunch of girls Abby didn't know. There were boys there, too.

Abby put down her fork and stared.

"What?" Sophia asked.

She couldn't answer. Next to Natalie, with his arm slung casually around her shoulder, was the boy she had bumped into in the hallway.

Chapter 3

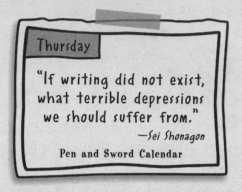

Thursday

"If writing did not exist,
what terrible depressions
we should suffer from."
—Sei Shonagon

Pen and Sword Calendar

It's just after lunch. I barely ate a bite. My stomach is clenched. My mind is reeling. My heart is thudding. It feels like it's about to leap out of my throat.

<u>What is happening to me????</u>
1. I am sick.
2. I am insane.
3. I am suffering from a rare, fatal disease.
4. That baked lasagna really WAS last year's leftovers.
5. I don't know.

Is this what depression feels like? If it is, it definitely feels terrible. I hope writing in my journal will help me.

I'm SO grateful for my journal. I'm SO glad I brought it to school today. I'm SO glad I can write in it, here in the back row of math class. I'm SO glad we have a substitute today and I don't have to pay attention.

Otherwise, how would I make sense of what I just saw?

He had his arm around Natalie's shoulder. And she acted as if it were the most ordinary thing in the world.

Take deep breaths. Count to twenty. Pinch hand. Check to see that Earth is still in its orbit.

Status of Universe:
1. Clock ticking.
2. Blackboard half-erased.
3. Chalk on floor.
4. Teacher shuffling papers.
5. Students pretending to study.

Universe seems normal. It's me that isn't.

Some Thoughts:
1. He knows Natalie.
2. Natalie knows him.
3. She knows his name.
4. He knows hers.
5. They are friends.
6. They are . . . never mind!

Some Questions:
1. Is Natalie interested in boys, even though she doesn't act like it?
2. Would she have a boyfriend and not tell me?
3. Why does it have to be HIM?
4. Why do I care?
5. Why am I so upset?

More Questions:
1. Can you know someone from looking in his eyes for a single moment?
2. Why do I think he might understand me?

3. Why do I want to look into his eyes again?

4. Is he thinking about me, too?

I hope that Sophia doesn't feel hurt that I ran out of the cafeteria without saying good-bye. Or without even finishing my sentence. One minute I was telling her that she was a good artist and ought to join the newspaper staff. The next minute I was gone.

When I see Sophia in art next period, I'll tell her that I had a stomachache.

It's NOT a lie. I feel sick to my stomach thinking about Natalie and that boy.

Anyone would. Right?

If this is a terrible depression, I hope it ends soon.

A sudden thought: I wonder if Bethany knows who HE is. She is Natalie's best friend. Natalie would tell _her_ if she had a boyfriend. And Bethany would tell _me_.

Chapter 4

Thursday | Still

"Everything must be like something, so what is this like?"

—E. M. Forster

Comparison Calendar

What is Ms. Bean's art class like?

First Impressions:
1. It is fun.
2. It is different.
3. It is creative.
4. It is not like school at all.
5. It is like . . .

Weird Coincidences:
1. Ms. Bean's art class is on Thursday, just like Ms. Bunder's writing class used to be.

2. Ms. Bean's last name also begins with <u>B</u>.

3. Ms. Bean is also young and teaching for the first time.

4. Her class seems unusual, just like writing class.

5. She might become my favorite teacher in middle school. Just like Ms. Bunder was my favorite teacher in elementary school.

But even if I love Ms. Bean's art class, and she reminds me of Ms. Bunder, I will ALWAYS love writing more than anything else in the world!

No one will ever replace Ms. Bunder!

"For our first project, we're going to do cubist self-portraits." As she spoke, Ms. Bean moved quickly and lightly from one side of the room to the other.

Abby closed her journal and slipped it into her backpack. She was glad to be in art class. A creative activity would take her mind off that boy.

Across from Abby, Sophia was drawing, as usual. She had made a quick sketch of the light fixture; now she was drawing a picture of the art teacher.

Ms. Bean was tiny and slender, with short dark hair and large brown eyes. She wore jeans and a blue sweater, pushed up at the elbows. She had a surprised expression, as if she didn't know how she had landed in a middle-school classroom.

"Here's a cubist portrait by Picasso." Ms. Bean held a book open to a picture of a woman. "Have any of you seen this before?"

Several of the students, including Sophia, nodded.

Abby stared at the picture. The woman's eyes bumped into each other. The nose was at an odd angle.

"Notice the different planes of the face," Ms. Bean said.

"It looks like a plane wreck," Mason said. "Or like someone folded up her face."

Ms. Bean smiled. "You understand."

"I do?" Mason said.

"Picasso was playing with the way we see," Ms. Bean said. "He wanted to open our minds to viewing reality in a different way. He wanted us to question our ideas about form, perspective, and geometry."

"No math!" someone groaned.

"It's, like, weird," Victoria sneered. "I mean, it's so totally ugly. Who'd want to look at *that*?" She scowled at the picture.

"This portrait makes you think, doesn't it?" the teacher said.

The meanest girl in sixth grade flipped back her dark hair. "It makes me think, like, I want to look into a mirror *right now*," Victoria retorted.

Ms. Bean ignored Victoria's rudeness. She nodded as if Victoria had said something brilliant. "That's exactly what I want you to do," she said.

"I knew that!" Victoria sputtered.

Abby hid a smile. It was rare that anyone got the best of Victoria. Ms. Bean might be a new teacher, but she handled Victoria like a pro.

Ms. Bean picked up a box and gave it to a boy next to her. "Take a mirror out of this box and look at your face. Study the lines, the angles, the shapes, and the colors. Then get some paper and paint and do your own cubist self-portrait."

Victoria stamped her foot. "We have to, like, paint ourselves like *that*?" she cried indignantly.

"There's no right or wrong in this class," Ms. Bean said. "There are just discoveries and invention."

Victoria didn't look happy. "What does *that* mean?"

"Shut up and start painting," Mason said.

"Like, shut up yourself, Mason," Victoria sniffed.

"Whatever you see or feel, put it on paper," Ms. Bean said. She darted to the blackboard and drew a large circle. "Explore your universe. And remember to have fun!" she added.

The class broke into an excited discussion.

Abby and Sophia exchanged glances.

"I think I'm going to *like* this class," Abby whispered.

"Me, too," Sophia whispered back.

Abby picked up the mirror that she had taken out of the box. She stared at her face. She wiggled her eyebrows, sucked in her cheeks, and pushed out her mouth. Then she examined herself from both the right and the left side.

The door of the classroom opened.

"You came for the papers?" Ms. Bean said. "I have them right here for you."

"Thanks," a boy said. "Do you have the key, too?"

Abby glanced up. She knew that voice. Her heart began to pound and her cheeks felt warm.

It was *him*.

Ms. Bean handed him a stack of papers and a key.

And then he was gone.

Who was he? What did she want from him, anyway?

She wondered if he had seen her making faces at herself in the mirror. Or hadn't he even noticed? Which was worse: to be seen or ignored?

Abby shook her head to get rid of these new and uncomfortable thoughts and picked up a paintbrush.

Everyone else had begun their self-portraits. In the back of the room, Mason was making bold strokes on a piece of paper.

Next to her, Sophia was lost in her drawing. She almost seemed like she was somewhere else. A few people talked quietly among themselves.

"Did you see that boy who just came in?" a girl named Aliya whispered at the next table. "He's the best musician in school."

Abby froze, her dripping brush held motionless in midair.

Another girl murmured something in reply.

"*Of course* he made the jazz band," Aliya said a little louder. "He plays the saxophone. He'll be the star soloist."

Aliya abruptly stopped talking. Ms. Bean was circulating through the class. She was watching the students work and offering advice.

Ms. Bean stopped at Aliya's table. She said a few words of encouragement, then moved on.

Abby glanced at Aliya, who was now concentrating fiercely on her portrait. She was a dancer and had a different group of friends from hers. Abby had never spoken to her.

So *he* was a musician. And not an ordinary one, but a star. Suddenly, he seemed beyond her reach.

Natalie was a star, too. In fifth grade, she had won the role of Peter Pan from the best actress and most popular girl in the class. Her name was Brianna, and it wasn't easy to compete against her. But Natalie had taken the role from her, anyway.

When Natalie decided to do something, she put her whole heart into it. She was probably a great musician, too. She might already have been accepted into the exclusive jazz band.

Why was it that *everyone* Abby knew was a star — except her?

Maybe Natalie and the boy practiced together. Maybe that was how they became friends . . . or boyfriend and girlfriend?

There was so much Abby didn't know anymore.

She sighed deeply, dipped her brush in the paint, and drew long, agitated swirls of color on the page.

Chapter 5

Once upon a time, I didn't tell secrets or listen to them. But now, all of a sudden, I've changed.

Yesterday I listened to Aliya talking about the saxophone player. She didn't reveal any secrets, but if she had, I would have LOVED it!

Then, a little later, I listened to Victoria gossiping with her friend Stacey. Stacey has a turned-up nose and sleek, bleached hair. She looks like a drowned rat.

Normally I shut out whatever they

say. But yesterday I gave them my complete attention. They were full of nasty secrets.

It's, Like, You Know, Another Totally, Yeah, Um, It's Like, Never Mind:
A transcript of a real, true, actual, factual conversation

Victoria: It's, like, he calls me, like, <u>all</u> the time, Stacey. It's so totally, like, you know how boyfriends are. . . .

Stacey: Like, yeah.

Victoria: Did you, like, hear about . . . ?

She lowered her voice and whispered a couple of names, which couldn't be heard across the room by a red-haired eavesdropper.

Stacey: Him? You mean, like, the one who just . . .

Victoria: Yes, him.

Stacey's eyes narrowed.

Victoria (sarcastic and nasty): The two of them are so <u>totally</u> cute.

Stacey: I didn't think she was the type.

Victoria: Like, she's different now, you know. It's, like, she totally changed, like, overnight. It all, like, happened this summer, you know.

That was all I heard. I inched closer, but I still missed the names. It really sounded like they were talking about Natalie and the star saxophone player.

<u>Were they?</u>

I want to know.
I have to know.
I need to know.
I am <u>DYING</u> to know.
I can't live with the suspense anymore.

On the way to school today, I asked Hannah, Casey, and Mason if they knew if Natalie had a boyfriend.
"Boyfriend?" Mason said. "<u>Natalie?</u>"
Casey shrugged, and Hannah gave me a funny look.
But then they all said no.

I asked Natalie's best friend, Bethany. She said no, too.

Bethany would know, wouldn't she? Or is she keeping a secret?

The only person I'd trust to give me the scoop is . . . Victoria.

I'm almost ready to ask her.

—

What is happening to me?

"You *have* to come with me," Sophia said. "I can't go in there alone."

The final bell had rung ten minutes ago. Abby and Sophia stood in front of the classroom where the newspaper staff was meeting.

"You can do it," Abby said encouragingly.

"*Please!*" Sophia begged. "Just this once."

Abby glanced inside the room. A group of students were chattering and laughing together.

"They look friendly," Abby said.

"They're *seventh- and eighth-graders*!" Sophia cried. "I'll be the only sixth-grader!"

"SO?" Abby said. "You might be the youngest, but I bet you're the most talented."

Sophia folded her arms across her chest.

"You don't need me," Abby insisted.

"Yes, I *do*." In a moment of uncharacteristic boldness, Sophia grabbed Abby's arm and pushed her into the room.

The entire newspaper staff looked up as the two girls entered.

Sophia turned deep red. She tried to back out of the room.

Abby put her hand on her friend's shoulder. "Sophia's an artist," she announced. "She's really good. She wants to be on the staff."

"Show us your work," said a tall girl with glasses perched on her wide nose.

Sophia hesitated. Then, looking deeply uncomfortable, she set a portfolio on the table.

The tall girl with glasses studied Sophia's drawings: kids and teachers, sunflowers and shoes, and geometric designs.

Then she broke into a wide smile. "We've found ourselves an artist!" she cried.

Sophia was surrounded by eagerly admiring seventh- and eighth-graders. For a moment, it looked like she was going to run, but she took a deep breath instead. Then she forced herself to answer a question.

Now she was talking with a boy about designing a

new logo for the newspaper. She almost seemed like she might enjoy herself.

Abby tiptoed out of the room. At the door, she turned and caught Sophia's eye. The two friends smiled at each other.

Abby walked down the corridor. Maybe she'd stop in the library and find a good book to read. Something to take her mind off that boy and Natalie.

Now that she had left the newspaper meeting, she was thinking about them again.

Abby glanced at her reflection in a window. It wasn't *too* bad, was it?

She didn't look like a fifth-grader anymore. She had pierced ears and a new haircut. She had a whole new wardrobe for middle school.

But would a boy notice her? Would *that* boy ever notice her?

Abby felt a pang of despair and then sharply dismissed it. She couldn't become one of those girls . . . those boy-crazy girls, like Crystal putting on layers of makeup in the locker room.

"I will never wear green eye shadow," Abby promised herself. "Or too much blush or shirts that are too small or . . ."

"Is that Abby Hayes?" It was Ms. Bean, heading toward her. She looked pleased to see Abby. "I was hoping to run into you."

"You know my name?" Abby said in astonishment. "After only one class?"

"I know all about you."

Abby stared at her in dismay. She hated it when teachers compared her to her older sisters.

"You know Eva and Isabel," she said, not trying to hide her disappointment.

"Eva and Isabel? Who are *they*?" Ms. Bean said. "A dear friend of mine told me all about you. She said you were one of her most imaginative students. She loved being your teacher, and she said I will, too."

"My fifth grade teacher?" Abby said in confusion. "Ms. Kantor?"

"Ms. Bunder," Ms. Bean said. "She says hello. She misses you."

"*Ms. Bunder!*" Abby repeated. "My favorite teacher of all time!"

Ms. Bean smiled. "I'm meeting her for coffee later. She'll be so happy to hear that you're in my class."

"Tell her I'm writing in my journal every day!"

"I will," Ms. Bean promised.

As she dialed the combination on her locker, Abby couldn't stop smiling. Ms. Bunder hadn't forgotten her. She had especially asked Ms. Bean to say hello to her.

Abby took out her coat and slammed her locker door shut. Maybe she'd write a letter to Ms. Bunder when she got home. There was a lot to tell her about sixth grade. If anyone would understand, it was Ms. Bunder.

Abby hurried toward the door. She couldn't wait to get home and get started. As she went around a corner, she heard laughing voices. Abby was just in time to see Natalie disappear down another hallway.

Natalie was accompanied by several boys carrying musical instrument cases. The tall one looked familiar.

It was HIM.

Without stopping to think, Abby ran down the hall after them.

Chapter 6

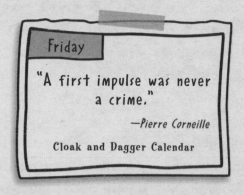

Friday

"A first impulse was never a crime."

—Pierre Corneille

Cloak and Dagger Calendar

I acted on my first impulse and followed Nalalie, the boy, and their friends. They disappeared into the auditorium. I slipped in through the door a few feet behind them and quickly sat down in the back of the auditorium.

They didn't notice me.

Question: If a first impulse isn't a crime, why do I feel so guilty?

<u>Notes from the Back of an Auditorium:</u>
It's very dark back here; only the stage

is lit up. I can barely see enough to write in my journal. Too bad I don't have a glow-in-the-dark purple pen! Or one with an attached miniature penlight.

They've all gone to the orchestra pit and started warming up their instruments.

Questions:
1. Is this the jazz band rehearsal?
2. Then Natalie _did_ make it after all? (Is that a question, or an answer?)
3. Why didn't she mention it?

Natalie has taken out her clarinet. He is blowing into a saxophone. Other kids have drums, flutes, and trombones. They're all playing at once, but not together. It sounds like a musical Tower of Babel.

Uh-oh! HE just looked in my direction. I slid way down in my seat. Thank goodness it's dark back here.

He better not guess that I've followed him. Otherwise I will die.

A man just arrived. He is wearing a sweater and blue jeans. His hair is long, white, and in a ponytail. He has a foreign accent. He doesn't look or sound ANYTHING like a teacher. He must be the famous musician who is directing the ensemble. He's just announced that the first Jazz Tones band rehearsal will begin in five minutes.

"And will someone _please_ turn on the lights?" he said.

Light is flooding the auditorium. I'm trying to make myself invisible.

Questions:
1. Why is light so BRIGHT?
2. How will I be able to leave without anyone noticing me?
3. What will I say when they ask why I'm here?

I only wanted to stay for a few minutes. I only wanted to see what _he_ and

Natalie were doing. I only wanted to know if they are boyfriend and girlfriend. Now I'm stuck here!

If I get up and leave, they'll ALL see me now.

HELP! I'M TRAPPED IN A MIDDLE-SCHOOL AUDITORIUM!

<u>Escape Plans:</u>

1. Crawl out of auditorium on hands and knees.

2. Hide between rows, wait until everyone leaves, and run out.

3. Borrow invisibility cloak.

Never mind. Will work on excuses for being here instead.

<u>Excuses, Excuses:</u>

1. I stopped to remove a pebble from my shoe.

2. I fell asleep in assembly two hours ago and just woke up.

3. I'm doing community service by picking up candy wrappers in the aisles.
4. I thought I was in the cafeteria.

What I Should Be Doing Instead of Thinking Up Excuses:
1. Hanging out with Hannah.
2. Avoiding my homework.
3. Arguing with my family.
4. Writing deep thoughts in my journal.
5. Daydreaming.
6. Eating chocolate cookies.

Interruption! We interrupt Abby's very important problems to let you know that the director is giving the Jazz Tones a pep talk. He is talking loudly enough so that I can hear every word. Even in the back of the auditorium.

Here is what he is saying:

"I've played in top bands all over Europe and the U.S.A. and I'm going to make you great," he says.

"I expect you to work your hardest, play your best, and give one thousand percent at all times. We are going to have the finest middle-school jazz ensemble this school — or any school — has ever seen."

Now he is reading off a list of their performances. They are giving concerts at an old people's home, in a pavilion downtown, and at several elementary schools. They are giving a holiday concert here at Susan B. Anthony. (It's only a month away!) And they're going to perform at a jazz festival in the spring, too.

Phew. It sounds scary.

Natalie and the boy don't look anxious at all. They look excited about giving one thousand percent at all times. Is that what makes them stars?

The band is getting ready to play.

I close my eyes to listen. It sounds good to me. But when I open my eyes, the director is shaking his head.

He says they can do much better. He's

going to help them achieve a level they never dreamed of. Now he's giving suggestions for each player.

They're doing it again. He's giving more suggestions.

And again.

And again.

And again.

And again . . .

Questions:

1. How do the Jazz Tones keep playing the same song over and over again?

2. How does the director always find something to improve?

3. Are the Jazz Tones ever going to play the piece the way he wants?

4. After hearing it one billion times (at least) will I ever forget this song?

5. Would the girl on the flute please move to the left so I can see the saxophone player?

HOORAY! The director says it's time to move on to something new. He says it's time for the saxophone solo. I can't believe it. I am SO lucky. Natalie just leaned over and said something to him.

I hope she's only wishing him luck.

He's onstage, with his saxophone. I love the way his hair falls down on his face. He has the most adorable smile in Susan B. Anthony Middle School. No, it's the cutest smile in the city — the state — the country — in the entire world!

(Help! Is this me writing this? Am I trapped in the mind of a green-eye-shadowed, tight-skirt-wearing alien?)

He's getting ready to play!

Wow.

I didn't know anyone in middle school could play like that.

He's good. I mean, he's really, really, really, really, really, really, REALLY good. He's so good he's great.

He IS a star.

The auditorium is so quiet it seems like all the musicians are holding their breath.

The director is listening intently.

* * *

He finished the solo. The director didn't have a single criticism. Then all the Jazz Tones jumped to their feet and cheered.

I did, too. I forgot where I was and what I was doing. I stood up and shouted with everyone else.

The rehearsal is over. Natalie turned around and saw me. She's coming toward me now. He's with Natalie. He's coming toward me, too.

HELP!!!! Now I'm _really_ trapped!
Question: **WHAT HAVE I DONE?**

Chapter 7

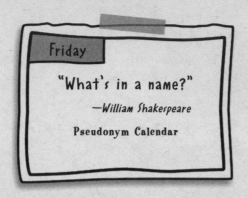

Friday

"What's in a name?"
—William Shakespeare

Pseudonym Calendar

<u>What's in HIS Name:</u>

1. Music
2. Incredibly bright eyes
3. A saxophone
4. A friendly smile

Natalie just introduced us. His name is Simon.

She said, "This is my friend Abby."

Simon acted like he was meeting me for the first time.

"It was nice of you to sit in on the rehearsal," he said. "What did you think of the Jazz Tones?"

"Um, you're so, uh, hardworking!" I stammered. "You had to play that song so many times!"

I wanted to sink through the floor.

"You look familiar," Simon said.

"Maybe you saw me in the supermarket," I blurted. "I mean, I help my dad with the shopping. I have to show him what kind of ice cream to buy or he gets the cheapest brands."

Simon smiled. His smile is REALLY nice.

I wished I could disappear. Couldn't I have found something more intelligent to say?

Good News: Simon has no memory of embarrassing accident.

(Maybe he won't remember my embarrassing babble?)

Bad News: I made no lasting impression on him.

<u>Good News:</u> He is an amazing musician.

<u>Bad News:</u> Why would he be interested in me?

<u>Good News:</u> Natalie thinks I came to the rehearsal to cheer her on.

<u>Bad News:</u> He thinks I'm there for her, too. (But isn't this good news, too?)

<u>Good News:</u> I don't know if Natalie and Simon are boyfriend and girlfriend.

<u>Bad News:</u> I don't know if Natalie and Simon are boyfriend and girlfriend.

<u>Good News:</u> I finally understand why I can't stop thinking about him.

<u>Is This Bad News or Good News:</u> I have a crush on Simon!

He's cute, he's talented, and he's super-nice! But he barely knows I exist.

"I can't believe you came to the rehearsal!" Natalie exclaimed. She gave Abby an enthusiastic hug. "You're *such* a great friend!"

"Uh, thanks," Abby said. She felt more like a great fraud than a great friend. But what else could she say?

She wasn't going to tell Natalie that she really had followed Simon. Not for a million dollars.

"It was so nice to have someone there cheering me on," Natalie continued, "even though I didn't see you until afterward. I'm sure it helped me play better."

"You were good." Abby picked up her backpack and zipped her coat. The two girls walked out of the school.

"Do you think so?" Natalie cried. She seemed like the old Natalie again. Her bored, sophisticated pose had vanished. She was friendly and open.

"It sounded like real music," Abby said. "I loved it, even though I don't usually listen to jazz. But I couldn't believe how many times the director made you repeat it."

Natalie sighed. "David is a perfectionist. At the audition, he said he only wanted the most dedicated musicians."

"When did you get so serious about the clarinet?" Abby asked.

"This summer. I went to music camp and did nothing but practice for six weeks." Natalie added, "Simon was there, too."

"He was?" Abby cried.

"*Of course* he was at music camp! He sleeps, eats, and breathes music. Didn't you notice? He's the best!"

"Yes, I noticed," Abby said, as nonchalantly as she could.

"Simon is going to be the star of the ensemble," Natalie said. "Talk about dedicated. He's been playing one instrument or another since he was three. Both his parents are music teachers."

Suddenly, Abby wished that *she* played an instrument, too. In second grade she had taken recorder lessons. In third, she had tried the violin. She had mastered "Twinkle, Twinkle, Little Star" and a few other tunes. Why hadn't she continued?

"He's incredible," Abby agreed. "I've never heard a sixth-grader play like that before."

"Simon's in seventh," Natalie said.

"Oh," Abby said with a shrug.

"He's one of those people who can do everything,"

Natalie said proudly. "He's talented at sports and school, too."

Simon was sounding more and more like Abby's older twin sisters, Eva and Isabel. They were outstanding at *everything*. There wasn't much air left to breathe for a younger sister who was normal and ordinary.

Would a gifted seventh-grade boy like Simon have a single reason to notice Abby? She was beginning to despair.

"Are you . . . are you . . ." Abby stammered.

"What?"

"His girlfriend?" Abby blurted before she could stop herself.

Natalie stared at her in shock. Then she said, "Of course not! Why can't a boy and girl be friends, without the whole world thinking they're boyfriend and girlfriend?"

"You're right," Abby apologized. Hadn't she hated being teased about her friendship with Casey?

She suddenly wondered if there was a girl who had a crush on Casey and was jealous of *her*. It was a funny thought.

"Here's where I turn," Natalie said. The friendliness and warmth she had shown after the audition was gone. She was once again her new sixth-grade self, cool and remote.

Abby wished she had never asked about Simon. "I'll see you tomorrow," she said.

Natalie nodded and waved and disappeared down the street.

Chapter 8

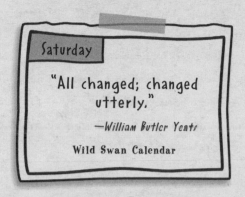

Yes, but <u>how</u>?

I feel different than I used to. It's hard to explain.

Having a crush is strange. I don't have any hope but I can't give up hope.

I hope that he will someday notice me. I hope that we will be friends. I hope that we will talk to each other. I hope. . . .

Hannah wants me to spend the afternoon at her house. Last week I would have loved it. This week I don't want to at all. I told her no.

I don't know what to do. I feel bored and restless. I feel like I'm going to jump out of my skin.

I wish I *could* jump out of my skin — I'd love to leave Abby for a few hours and try being someone else.

Like Natalie, who's gifted at music — and cool and sophisticated, too.

Or I could be one of my SuperSisters, brilliant like Isabel or an athletic star like Eva.

Or Hannah, who's so friendly that everyone loves her. Or Bethany, who knows everything about animals. Or even shy Sophia, who has so much talent at drawing.

Right now, I'd like to be anyone but me!

"Don't you have anything to do?" Abby's mother said to her daughter. "You've been moping around the house all morning."

"I'm *not* moping," Abby said. She was lying on the couch, staring up at the ceiling. "I'm *thinking*."

"Ah," her mother said.

It was eleven in the morning. Olivia Hayes had already jogged, worked on notes for a law brief, and done three loads of laundry.

"What does your room look like?" her mother asked.

"Purple," Abby said.

"I know it's purple," her mother said patiently. "I meant, is it *clean*?"

"Sort of." Abby flung one arm over her forehead. "I vacuumed and picked up the dirty clothes."

"Good. Is your homework done?"

"Mostly."

"Chores?"

Abby sighed. "Yes, Mom."

Olivia picked up a magazine someone had dropped on the floor. "Well, then, you're free to mope in peace."

"I'm not *moping*," Abby said again.

"You're thinking," her mother repeated absentmindedly. She glanced around the room and then said to no one in particular, "I have to pick up the dry cleaning before lunch."

Abby watched her hurry out of the room. Her mother's busy life seemed so *important*.

Even if she was only picking up the dry cleaning, Olivia Hayes was always purposeful, focused, and energetic.

Abby's sister Isabel shuffled into the living room in big white furry slippers. She was still wearing her blue fleece pajamas.

Isabel must have slept late. That was unusual.

"Hey, what's up, sis?" Abby said.

Isabel sat down next to her on the couch. "I've been studying since six A.M.," she announced. "I haven't even stopped to get dressed. I wrote a world history essay, did my French homework, studied for a bio exam, and took notes on a short story for English class."

"Is that *all*?" Abby groaned. Her family worked in their sleep. Didn't anyone ever lie around and stare at the ceiling?

"Isn't that enough?" Isabel asked. "So how's sixth grade going? How are your classes?"

"Fine." It was as if Isabel hadn't seen her in weeks, Abby thought. And they lived in the same house.

Isabel studied her fingernails. They were painted lime green. "Eva met the cutest boy in the cafeteria yesterday," she confided.

"Oh, yeah?" Abby perked up. "Who is he?"

"He's not in any of her classes. We found out he's a junior in high school."

"Wow," Abby said. She actually had something in common with Eva — aside from the same last name, of course. They both liked older men.

"She's thinking of asking him to a dance next week," Isabel said.

"She'd *do* that?" Abby was amazed at her sister's courage.

Isabel shrugged. "Why not?" She leaned back on the couch. "Are there any cute boys at Susan B. Anthony this year?"

"Of course not!" To her embarrassment, Abby began to blush.

Her sister looked closely at her. Abby couldn't meet her eyes.

"I'm not one of those girls who thinks about boys all the time, you know." Abby sat up and folded her arms across her chest.

Isabel patted her shoulder in a reassuring way. "Don't worry. I know what it's like. You can tell me."

"There's nothing to tell," Abby snapped. She hated it when Isabel acted like she was twenty years older and had the wisdom of the universe.

"Or maybe you want to ask me something."

Abby scowled at her. Isabel was irritating, but she *did* know more about boys than Abby.

"I might ask you a question," she finally said. "But it's not about me!"

"Go ahead," Isabel said with a small smile.

Abby took a deep breath. "Did you ever have a crush on a boy who didn't know you existed?"

"It happens all the time," Isabel said. "Let me tell you, I make them notice me."

"How?"

"By not doing anything."

Abby sighed. Isabel wasn't making any sense at all. Sometimes she was too brilliant for her own good — or anyone else's.

"How do you make sure he notices you without doing anything?"

"That's the art of it," Isabel said. She breathed on her fingernails and polished them with a tissue.

" 'To thine own self be true,' " she added, throwing some Shakespeare into the conversation. "Always be yourself."

"I knew that," Abby said sarcastically. Why had she even opened her mouth?

Isabel was the top student in her grade, class president, star of the debating team, and had won every scholarship award in the school.

Of course she didn't have to do anything! Of course she only had to "be herself." It was impossible NOT to notice her.

Why did her older sisters have to outdo Abby in *everything*? They were even overachievers in crushes!

Abby would *never* follow Eva's example and ask Simon to a dance. She could just imagine his baffled expression.

"Sorry, I can't," he might say. "I'm too busy being a serious musician and an outstanding student athlete." If Abby was lucky, he'd remember that she was Natalie's friend.

And if Abby followed Isabel's advice, he'd never notice her at all.

Chapter 9

Sunday

"Somewhere, something incredible is waiting to be known."
—Carl Sagan
Planet Earth Calendar

Or some<u>one</u> incredible is waiting to be known?
Like ME?
Or Simon?

I can't think about Simon anymore or my brain is going to explode.
I will call a friend instead.

Abby's Call-a-Friend-Before-I-Go-Crazy Log:
1. Hannah: no answer.
2. Casey: at basketball game.

3. Natalie: has to practice clarinet and clean her room.

4. Bethany: taking care of the animal kingdom.

5. Mason: has to babysit his cousins.

6. Sophia: drawing. She's coming over as soon as she finishes.

HOORAY! Three cheers for Sophia! I hope she will cheer me up.

"Your room is purple!" Sophia exclaimed as she entered Abby's room. She twirled around to take it all in. "I wish I could do *my* room like this."

"What's it like?" Abby asked. This was the first time she and Sophia had spent time together outside of school.

"It's dull, boring, pale blue wallpaper." Sophia sighed. "My mother says it's too expensive to change. So I've tacked up drawings on all the walls."

"Like an art gallery."

"I also put up posters of my favorite movie stars."

"*Boy* movie stars?"

Sophia blushed.

Abby glanced at her walls, imagining Simon's face

there. But where would she get his picture? And what would she say if her family saw it?

Sophia put a sketch pad down on Abby's desk. "I brought my pad so I could draw you. Is that okay?"

"Yes!" Abby cried. "That's *awesome*. No one has ever drawn a picture of me before. What do I have to do?"

Sophia opened a case of pencils and charcoal sticks. "Nothing special. Just act natural. Be yourself."

Be yourself. That phrase again. Isabel had said it to her yesterday. With a sigh, Abby sat down cross-legged on the bed.

Sophia settled herself in a chair. She picked up a pencil, opened her sketch pad, and began to draw.

"'Be yourself' is everyone's all-purpose advice, isn't it?" Abby mused. "When I ask my parents or sisters a serious question, that's what they always say."

"I know what you mean," Sophia said.

"'Just be yourself, dear,'" Abby repeated. "How am I supposed to be myself when things are changing so fast that I don't know who I am anymore?

"And besides," she added, "you don't always get what you want by being yourself. Sometimes you need to be someone else. But how do you get the courage to do that?"

Sophia nodded. "I was terrified of walking into that newspaper staff meeting. But then I forced myself to do it and I loved it."

Abby leaned back against a pillow. "That's so great!"

"I couldn't have done it without you," Sophia said.

"*You* dragged *me* into the meeting," Abby reminded her.

The bedroom door suddenly flew open.

It was Abby's younger brother, Alex. He wore rumpled pants and a shirt that were suspiciously similar to yesterday's pajamas.

"You didn't knock, Alex!" Abby scolded him. "And get dressed already. It's the middle of the afternoon."

Alex ignored her. "You have a visitor."

"Yes, I have a visitor." Abby sighed. "*Duh*. Can't you see there's an artist at work? Go away."

"You have *another* visitor. Hannah's here. She'll be right up." Alex stuck out his tongue and slammed the door.

Sophia put down her pencil. "I can leave."

"You don't have to go," Abby said. "It's just Hannah. And anyway, you haven't finished my picture."

"I'll finish it another time," Sophia said quickly.

"Hannah's really friendly," Abby said.

"But I . . ." Sophia began.

Before she could say another word, the door opened and Hannah came in.

"Abby!" she cried. "I heard your message and tried to call, but the line was busy. So I came right over."

Then she saw Sophia. Her smile widened.

"Hi, I'm Hannah," she said. "You're Sophia, aren't you? It's great to finally get a chance to know you."

Sophia mumbled a few barely audible words in reply.

If Abby hadn't known how shy Sophia was, she would have thought that she was unfriendly.

Hannah looked confused.

Abby had a sinking feeling that her two friends weren't going to get along. And they were both in her room.

It was the *last* thing in the world that she wanted to worry about right now.

Chapter 10

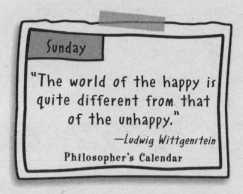

Sunday

"The world of the happy is quite different from that of the unhappy."

—Ludwig Wittgenstein

Philosopher's Calendar

The world of Hannah is quite different from that of Sophia.

My two friends together were like two opposite worlds in one tiny purple room.

Hannah's World:
Sat down on bed.
Made self at home.
Talked to me and Sophia.

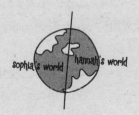

Sophia's World:
Picked up sketchbook and clutched it to chest.

Didn't say anything.
Looked like she wanted to run.

Collision of the Two Worlds:
Hannah asked Sophia a question.
Sophia mumbled an answer.
Hannah repeated her question.
There was a long moment of awkward silence.

Help! It's My Room and I Have to Save the Universe:
No one said anything.
Hannah was looking curiously at Sophia and then at me.
Sophia looked very upset.
It was an awful moment.
I had to say SOMETHING.

What I Might Have Said:
To Hannah: Next time, call first.
To Sophia: You miss a lot by being shy and scared all the time.
To both: It's not my fault if you don't like each other.

To both again: I hate getting stuck in the middle of your misunderstanding.

And finally: Today I need you to understand ME.

But I didn't say any of that.

Instead I blurted, "Let's talk about boys!"

Why Did I Say THAT?

Hannah looked puzzled.

Sophia looked unhappy.

Hannah said, "Why should we talk about boys?"

Sophia said nothing.

Making Things Worse:

I said, "Um, well, I don't know. I just thought we could, um, talk about crushes, and, uh, stuff like that."

"I don't get crushes," Hannah said firmly, as if they were a kind of flu.

"You don't? Ever?"

A "Crushing" Conversation:

Hannah shook her head. "Boys are just people. People like us. What's the big deal?"

"I don't get it, either," I lied. "But aren't they a lot different from us?"

"How so?" Hannah asked.

What Do I Say NOW?

It was my turn to be silent.

Sophia to the Rescue:

Sophia shifted in her chair. "I've had crushes since I was five," she mumbled.

"You have?" I cried. "Since you were five?"

"I always like some boy or other," Sophia admitted in a whisper.

"And then . . . ?" I asked.

"Nothing. I'm just romantic."

"I'm not!" Hannah said. "At least not yet. What about you, Abby?"

"Me?" My face started turning red. "I, well, I . . ."

Sophia glanced at me, as if she suddenly understood. But she didn't say anything.

(Thank you, thank you, thank you, Sophia. You will receive the "Silence is Golden" award in the <u>Hayes Book of World Records</u>.)

"I just don't get this crush stuff," Hannah repeated.

<u>Hannah Changes the Subject:</u>
"What's in that notebook?" she suddenly asked Sophia.

Sophia clutched it more tightly. "Uh, I, um . . ."

"She's a really good artist!" I said to Hannah.

"Show Hannah your drawings!" I said to Sophia.

"I'd love to see them! Please?" Hannah asked.

Sophia didn't move. I held my breath.

Then she put her sketchbook on my desk and opened it up.

<u>A New Quote. Just Because, Why Not?</u>

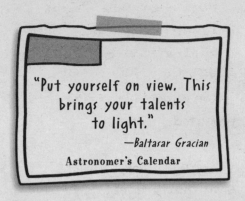

"Put yourself on view. This
brings your talents
to light."
—Baltasar Gracian
Astronomer's Calendar

Does this quote need ANY explanation?

Sophia put herself on view. She opened
her sketchbook and brought her talents to
light.

Hannah couldn't believe how good the
pictures were.

She asked Sophia lots of questions and
Sophia answered them, sort of.

I don't think they'll ever be friends, but
the next half hour until Sophia left was
okay.

Finally, Hannah and I were alone.

We went down to the kitchen to get a snack. We found a plate of freshly baked cookies on the table. Everything was fine. I started to relax again.

Until Hannah asked, "Why are you so interested in crushes all of a sudden?"

"I'm not, really," I lied. "It's this friend of Natalie's who . . ." My voice trailed off. I didn't know what I was going to say, anyway, but I couldn't go on.

So I changed the subject. "Didn't you notice how shy Sophia is? I was just trying to start a conversation."

At least it was halfway true.

"Even though she's shy, her pictures speak for her," Hannah said. "She's so talented."

I nodded in agreement.

Then she added, "I'm glad you're not interested in crushes. I'd hate it if you turned into one of those boy-crazy girls. It's not you, Abby."

"No, it isn't," I lied again, looking her straight in the eye.

Now I know that I can _never_ tell

Hannah about Simon. She'd never understand.

It's bad enough having a crush, but it's worse not being able to admit it to your best friend.

Chapter 11

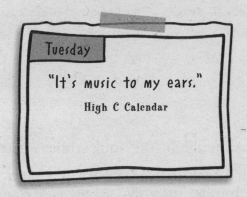

Tuesday

"It's music to my ears."

High C Calendar

This morning, Natalie came up to me on the way to first-period class. She invited me to sit in on the Jazz Tones rehearsal today.

She was really grateful when I said yes.

"You wouldn't mind, Abby? I have to play a short solo and I'm scared. David is really tough."

I was surprised to hear that Natalie was scared. I was also flattered that she wanted me there.

I'd sit in on a rehearsal for Natalie
anytime, but now I get to watch Simon,
too. Can it get any better?

This is music to my ears!

Hooray, hooray, **hooray**! Or
should I sing "tra la la" instead?

"Tra la la!"

"Sit in the middle of the auditorium," Natalie told
Abby. "That's where the acoustics are best."

"I'll be rooting for you!" Abby said. She found a
seat in the center of the auditorium. Then she sat
down and waited for the rehearsal to begin.

The musicians were warming up. Simon was blowing into his saxophone; Natalie was cleaning her
clarinet with a long silk cloth.

Abby was officially there for Natalie, but she
hoped that no one would ask if there was *another*
reason she kept coming to the Jazz Tones rehearsals.
And she especially hoped that no one would figure
out her crush on Simon.

If only she were a musician in the band! Then
she'd have a reason to show up at every single rehearsal.

Abby took out her journal. Last night she had
written Simon's name at the back of the book in let-

ters so tiny as to be almost unreadable. She hoped that no one would ever find out that she had spent more than an hour writing a boy's name over and over in her journal.

She flipped to today's page and sat for a moment, thinking.

But before she could write a single word, someone slipped into the seat next to her.

Abby slammed her journal shut.

"Don't be alarmed! It's just me," Hannah said with a friendly smile. "I've been looking for you. Bethany told me you were here. Will you walk home with me?"

"Sorry, I can't. I promised Natalie I'd stay. She's playing a solo."

Hannah stared at the musicians. "Who's that man with the white ponytail?" she asked.

"He's the band director." Abby took a breath. "His name is David. He's from another country, but I forget which one."

"Wow. Cool," Hannah said. She leaned forward in her seat and waved to Natalie.

But Natalie didn't see her. She was talking to Simon. He was pointing to her clarinet. She was laughing.

"She's really friendly with that boy," Hannah commented.

"She's *not!*"

Hannah looked curiously at her.

"I mean, she just knows him from music camp," Abby said quickly. "They're not boyfriend and girlfriend. That's all."

Hannah stood up. "I wish I could stay and cheer Natalie on, too, but I can't." She picked up her backpack, said good-bye to Abby, and walked out of the auditorium.

With a sigh of relief, Abby slumped into the chair.

She hoped that Hannah hadn't guessed how she felt about Simon. She was glad that Hannah had left before she said something to make her suspicious.

There was a commotion near the stage. Several people were talking at once. David was upset.

"We have only half the equipment we need," he announced in frustration. "Someone will have to go get the janitor. But I don't want any of you to leave, even for five minutes. You all need to be here *now*. We don't have a lot of rehearsal time before our first concert."

Natalie spoke up. Abby couldn't hear what she

was saying, but suddenly, all the Jazz Tones were staring in her direction. So was David.

"You there!" he called.

Abby looked around. There was no one else in the auditorium. "Me?" she said.

"Yes, you. Curly Red! Will you find the janitor for us?"

Chapter 12

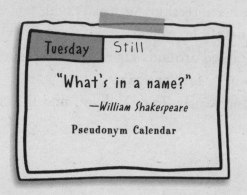

Tuesday | Still

"What's in a name?"

—William Shakespeare

Pseudonym Calendar

I know I used this quote less than a week ago. SO WHAT?

What's in my name? Abby is a good name (unless someone calls me Abigail, which I <u>hate</u>. It makes me think of a lady with white hair in a colonial dress sitting at a spinning wheel).

Abby. My name is Abby.

Abby. Abby. Abby. Abby. Abby. Abby.
Abby. Abby. Abby. Abby. Abby. Abby.
Abby.

Get it???

My name is Abby. NOT Curly Red.

But anyway, I still went to find the
janitor. Why? Because of Simon, of course.

"Make yourself necessary
to someone."
—Ralph Waldo Emerson

Wise Advice Calendar

Yes, another quote. Just because. And
like I said, I used the last one twice.

I found the janitor mopping the floors in
the guidance office and gave him the message about the missing equipment.

He said he'd take care of it right away.

I ran back to the auditorium. The Jazz Tones were playing their first piece. David's white ponytail bounced up and down as he conducted.

"He's on his way!" I said when they had put down their instruments.

"You're a lifesaver, Curly Red!" David said. He fished in his pockets and brought out a pile of quarters. "Will you get me a cola from the soda machine? I forgot to get it and I desperately need something to drink. Thank you, you're a love."

I got David a soda.

Then he asked me if I would write each band member's name on a separate folder. He handed me the folders, the list of names, and papers to put in each one.

It wasn't exactly exciting. In fact, this was the kind of work I normally hated doing. I felt like one of those Siberian huskies with a keg of lifesaving refreshment around her neck.

But I was in the front row, near Simon. <u>Anything</u> was worth it for him.

I stopped writing names on folders to listen to Natalie play her solo.

At the end, David said, "Well done." He only had a few suggestions to make. I gave her a thumbs-up.

Then David asked me if I would go to the back of the auditorium and listen to the Jazz Tones play.

I tried to listen carefully so I could answer David's questions about the sound. It took a lot of concentration. But he seemed pleased with my answers.

It was nice to be necessary to the Jazz Tones. They cheered when the janitor showed up. David called me a lifesaver. Natalie kept smiling at me. Simon looked at me twice, which made it all worthwhile.

"You can help us out if you want," David said to me at the end of rehearsal. "There's no title, no money, you'll do whatever needs doing, and all you'll get in return is lots of appreciation."

"And an invitation to the Jazz Tones party!" Natalie spoke up.

"What party?" David joked. "This is a working ensemble."

"I'm having an after-concert party at my house next month," Simon explained. "The entire band is invited."

"So?" David asked.

I didn't think I'd get invited to Simon's party if I didn't help out. And helping out gave me a reason to show up at rehearsals. How else would I get to hang around Simon?

"Yes, I'll do it," I said.

I couldn't believe what I was getting myself into.

David shook my hand. "Welcome on board, Curly Red."

"Abby. My name is Abby."

"I'm terrible with names," David apologized. "I try to think up nicknames I can remember instead."

The band groaned.

David has given them all nicknames.

Simon is Simon Says.

Natalie reminds David of a 1920s movie star. He calls her Flapper. One of the other musicians is Einstein. And there's another girl with white-blond hair who he calls Snow Queen.

I <u>hate</u> Curly Red. Why can't he call me Purple Hayes? Maybe I'll suggest it to him next time.

Something REALLY wonderful happened after the rehearsal.

A few of the kids decided to go to the Snowy Owl Café for hot chocolate. Natalie invited me along!

Chapter 13

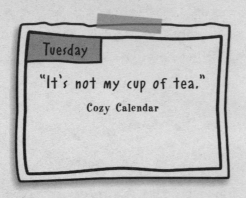

Tuesday

"It's not my cup of tea."

Cozy Calendar

It's my cup of hot chocolate!
Or my cup of steamed milk.
Or my cup of espresso?

The Jazz Tones are having hot chocolate with whipped cream at the Snowy Owl Café. Except for Natalie. She's having an espresso.

I'm drinking a cherry steamer. That's foamy hot milk with syrup. There were so many syrup flavors — cherry, vanilla, almond, chocolate, hazelnut, raspberry, orange, mint, and kiwi — that it took me forever to decide.

When I went back to the table, the Jazz Tones were throwing around words like interval, cadence, tempo, fortissimo, and andante. They were talking about musicians and composers I'd never heard of. It was like listening to a foreign language.

I sipped at my cherry steamer and wished they'd say something I understood.

Finally, they started talking about David. They all think he's tough but fair. They like him a lot, except for the nicknames.

NO ONE in the band likes the nicknames.

A Short Conversation About Nicknames:

Natalie: "When he calls me Flapper, I feel like a pinball machine. Or a penguin."

Simon (smiling at her): "You don't look like one. At all."

Me: Silently made plans to straighten my hair, cut it short, and dye it black. Made mental note to get rid of clogs and buy leather shoes like Natalie's instead.

Einstein: "Flappers were glamorous in the

1920s. Maybe David means it as a compli-
ment, Natalie."

Natalie: "Couldn't David call me something more modern?"

Simon: "I hate 'Simon Says.' It reminds
me of being teased when I was a little
kid. They used to yell 'Simon says!' on the
playground."

Natalie (hits him playfully): "How could
anyone tease you, Simon? You're so nice!"

Me: Didn't say anything. Wished I could
joke around with Simon like that.

Alicia (the drummer): "When David calls
me Snow Queen, I feel cold."

Einstein: "My nickname is okay. Sort of. I
mean, how can I complain about being
named for a genius?"

They all agreed that Einstein got the best
nickname.

Einstein: "My real name is Lucas."

Simon: "But you seem like an Einstein. Do
you mind if we call you that?"

Einstein shrugged modestly.

Me: "Maybe you should think of a nickname for David."

Simon smiled at me. "What a good idea."

They all started thinking of nicknames for David.

"Jazz Man," Natalie said.

"Ponytail," said Simon.

"B.D., short for Band Director," Alicia said.

"Nickname," Einstein said.

"Toot Toot?" I said, thinking of his trombone.

Everyone laughed at that. And Simon said, "Pretty funny." I felt so happy. Finally, I had gotten him to notice me.

We were thinking of more nicknames when Natalie looked at the clock, jumped up, said "I'm out of here," and grabbed her coat.

She practically vanished. She left so quickly that I didn't even realize that she was gone.

When I looked out the window, I saw her running across the street.

Simon watched her go. "I hope she doesn't get in trouble," he said, frowning. "Her parents are kind of strict."

How does _he_ know that?

A few minutes later, Einstein and Alicia left, too. Then, all of a sudden, it was only me and Simon.

When I realized that we were sitting by ourselves in a café, I started feeling REALLY nervous.

But Simon said, in a very friendly way, "Would you like a ride home? I'm going to call my parents." He pulled out a cell phone.

"Do you play an instrument?" Simon asked Abby as they drove away from the Snowy Owl.

"Um, I played the triangle in a school play in kindergarten," she said. "In third grade, I did 'Twinkle, Twinkle, Little Star' on the violin."

Abby tried to end with a joke. "Since then, I've mastered the kazoo."

"'Twinkle, Twinkle'?" Simon repeated as if he couldn't quite believe it. "And what's your favorite tune on the kazoo?"

Abby was too mortified to answer.

"Do I turn here?" Simon's father asked Abby.

"Yes," Abby said, grateful for the interruption. "Make a right at the next traffic light. Then go straight for two blocks. We're the second house on the right."

After a minute, Simon said, in a different tone of voice, "How do you like sixth grade? Are you shocked at how much everyone has changed?"

Yes, and me most of all, Abby thought. But she didn't say it. "It *is* strange," she admitted. "It's like going through the Looking Glass."

"Who are Tweedledum and Tweedledee?" Simon asked.

Abby looked at him in surprise. "The two sixth-grade math teachers."

Simon burst out laughing. "Perfect!"

The car pulled into Abby's driveway. The ride was over, just as their conversation was beginning.

Simon smiled at her. "See you next rehearsal, Abby."

Abby lingered, not wanting the moment to end. Her eyes met his for a moment, then she jumped out of the car and waved good-bye.

In the driveway, Alex and a friend were tossing a

ball back and forth. They stared at Abby and snick-ered.

"Is that your *boyfriend*, Abby?" Alex said loudly.

"Alex!" Abby's face burned. Behind her, the car pulled away. Abby didn't dare look back. She turned and ran into the house.

Chapter 14

Tuesday

"The less said, the better."

—Jane Austen

Strong, Silent Calendar

There is very little to say.

Except that I wish that Alex had said
<u>nothing</u>.

I want to hide under my bed
for the rest of my life. If I
turn into a pile of dust and get
swept into a pail, I don't care.
I will never forgive Alex. He has
ruined my life, with one little
word. And everything was going
so well!!!

Did Simon hear him? What did he think?

Does he know I have a crush on him? I wish I could disappear. Why did Alex have to be there?

WHY? WHY? WHY?

Chapter 15

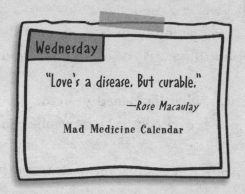

Wednesday

"Love's a disease. But curable."

—Rose Macaulay

Mad Medicine Calendar

<u>What Disease Is Love?</u>
1. Insanity
2. Measles
3. Heart attack
4. Fever
5. Confusion

This morning I feel <u>awful</u>.

<u>Cure for Disease of Love:</u>
?????????????????????????????????
1. Stop thinking about Simon.

2. Stop worrying about whether he heard Alex call him my boyfriend.

3. Stop imagining conversations with him.

4. Stop writing his name in my journal.

"Did you hear what happened yesterday in school?" Hannah asked excitedly as she came out of her house.

"No," Abby said, adjusting a strap on her backpack. "What?"

"A whole group of kids got sent home after first period to change their clothes," Hannah said. "They wore 'Down With Homework' T-shirts."

Abby smiled. She matched her pace to Hannah's as the two girls headed toward middle school.

"Did you see them?" she asked.

"No." Hannah stopped to shake a pebble out of her shoe. "I heard it was a group of seventh-graders."

Abby wondered if Simon was one of them. Probably not. Someone would have mentioned it at the Snowy Owl.

"Did you hear what I just said, Abby?"

"Um, no," Abby said. "Sorry."

"I said, I'm going to join the stage crew," Hannah repeated.

Abby stared at her. "When did you decide that?"

"Just a day ago," Hannah said. "They need kids to build and paint sets for the play. Do you want to join us after school?"

"I'm going to the Jazz Tones rehearsal."

Now it was Hannah's turn to be surprised. "Have you learned to play an instrument overnight?"

"I *wish*!" Abby said. "The only instrument I know how to use is a pen."

Hannah frowned. "So why do you keep going to rehearsals?"

"I, um, do stuff for the director," Abby explained. "I run around and get him sodas, file papers, and find the janitor when he needs him. I'm sort of like, uh, a team mascot, or something."

"Sounds like fun," Hannah said dubiously.

"It is!" Abby said. "I love it!"

"Are you *sure* that you don't want to build sets with me?" Hannah pleaded. "It's going to be so much fun. And we're having a cast party at the end."

"Sorry." Abby shook her head. "I'm already committed."

The two girls crossed the street and made their way over a bridge. They were almost at the school.

"I don't get it," Hannah said. She seemed confused. "Wouldn't you rather do something more creative?"

"It's creative enough. . . ." Abby's voice trailed off. How could she explain it without telling Hannah about Simon?

"You should have joined the newspaper staff with Sophia," Hannah said. "I can see you as an ace reporter."

"I didn't want to."

"O-*kay*." Hannah took a breath. "And you're *really* happy fetching sodas for some director?"

"I'm happy," Abby said defiantly. So what if being David's assistant wasn't creative? She was needed. And she was *there* — where Simon was. "I'm learning about acoustics and music, and where the janitor hangs out after school, and all sorts of things."

Hannah was silent.

Abby wondered why she had to defend herself to Hannah. Wasn't her best friend supposed to understand and accept her as she was?

"I don't know you anymore," Hannah finally said.

"No, you don't," Abby agreed.

The two girls stared at each other. Hannah's eyes slowly filled with tears. Then she broke away from Abby and ran into the school.

Chapter 16

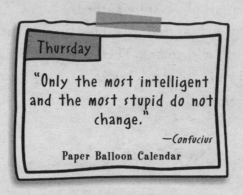

Thursday

"Only the most intelligent and the most stupid do not change."

—Confucius

Paper Balloon Calendar

I am neither "most intelligent" nor "most stupid." And I'm changing.

Question: If it's normal to change, why do I feel so awful?

Question: Why did I hurt Hannah's feelings?

Question: Why doesn't she know who I am anymore?

Question: What would happen if I told her the truth?

Question: What if I told her about Simon . . . and she thought that I was silly or crazy or dumb?

Question: What if she didn't like me any-more?

Question: What if she didn't want to be my friend?

It's easier and safer to say nothing, and to pretend that I'm not really changing.

Question: Or is it really?

HELP!

Hannah and I have been friends since the moment we met. If it wasn't for Hannah, I would have been _much_ more miser-able when Jessica, my former best friend, went to live with her father in Oregon. Hannah and I have had so many good times together.

I wish I hadn't hurt Hannah's feelings. How will I make it up to her? Everything is getting more and more confusing and com-plicated!

I wish I wasn't changing so much. Or

I wish that Hannah was changing, too,
just like me.

Ms. Bean circulated in the art room, looking at everyone's work. Sometimes she made a suggestion, but mostly she smiled or said a few words of encouragement.

"Great!" she said to Abby.

Abby had drawn her hair in wild blocks of purple curls. Her nose looked like a pyramid; her eyes were like marbles. She dipped her brush in paint and sketched a stage in the background.

She drew musical notes in the air. Then she wrapped words around her head like a scarf. She put a large journal under her feet and a purple pen in her hand.

"I *like* it," Sophia said. "It's kind of surreal, too."

"What's that mean?" Abby said.

"Not realistic, but more like a dream," Sophia explained. "Your portrait is dreamlike."

"Is it a nightmare?" Abby said. Her life felt like one lately. She and Hannah hadn't spoken since yesterday.

Abby put down her brush. She walked over to Ms. Bean. "I'm done with my self-portrait," she announced. "It's drying now."

Ms. Bean nodded. Then she said, "Abby, since you're finished early, will you take something to the library for me?"

"All right," Abby said. She wondered if the words "errand runner" were tattooed across her forehead.

Ms. Bean scrawled a few words on a piece of paper. "Here's your pass," she said. "Don't get lost."

"*Lost?*" Abby glanced at her teacher. Was she serious?

"I'm kidding," Ms. Bean said. "It's my sense of humor. Sometimes people don't get it."

"I know what you mean," Abby said.

Lately she felt as if she couldn't get through to anyone. At least, not in the right way. First it was Simon and now Hannah.

They were the two people she liked best. How had *that* happened?

Abby handed a file to the librarian's assistant. "I'm supposed to pick up a magazine for Ms. Bean, too," she said.

"Here you are," the assistant said.

"Thank you," Abby said. As she turned to leave, Simon walked out of the stacks. He had a book under his arm.

Abby's heart started pounding wildly. He didn't

seem to see her. Or maybe he was pretending not to see her?

"Um, hi," she finally said.

Simon seemed surprised. And then he smiled. "Hi, Abby."

"Hi," Abby repeated.

Right now, Sophia was a social butterfly compared to her.

"I'm glad I ran into you."

"You *are*?" Abby breathed.

Simon handed his library book to the librarian.

Abby wondered if she should say something about Alex. Or should she say nothing?

If Simon had heard Alex yelling "boyfriend," it didn't appear to bother him. Maybe this was the sort of thing that happened to him all the time.

"We're having pizza at my house tomorrow after rehearsal," he said. "You're invited."

"I *am*?"

"Of course," he said. "Can you come?"

Abby nodded wordlessly.

"Great," Simon said. "I'll see you later, then."

As Abby walked back to the art room, she replayed the conversation over and over.

Simon had invited her to his house. And he hadn't mentioned Alex's outburst.

That was good.

On the other hand, she had only spoken in words of three letters or less.

That wasn't good.

But now she was invited to his house on Friday after school. With any luck, she'd be less tongue-tied. She'd show him who she really was.

Abby handed Ms. Bean the magazine. "Shall I start another self-portrait?" she asked.

The art teacher glanced at the clock. "If you want. I don't mind if you use the remaining time to write. Just don't disturb the others who are still working."

"I won't!" Abby said. "Thank you!" None of her teachers had ever given her permission to write in her journal during class. She usually had to hold it on her lap and write secretly.

Abby opened the journal and wrote a few words about Simon. Then suddenly, she closed it and took out a piece of lined paper instead.

She began writing a letter to Hannah.

Chapter 17

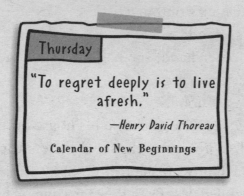

Thursday

"To regret deeply is to live afresh."

—Henry David Thoreau

Calendar of New Beginnings

Dear Hannah, I know I hurt your feelings and I am really, really, really, really sorry. REALLY! You are my best friend. I hope you're not mad at me. Love, Abby

Dear Abby, You're my best friend, too. I'm sorry we had a fight. I've been feeling rotten all day. I guess I don't understand some of the things you're doing. But you'll always be my friend, no matter what. I hope you're not mad at ME! Love, Hannah

Dear Hannah, Of course I'm not mad at you. I shouldn't have snapped at you. It's just that . . . that . . . well, can

you understand that I HAVE to do this stuff for the Jazz Tones right now? I need to and I can't explain any more.
Love, Abby

Dear Abby, Whatever you do is fine with me, as long as we're friends. Love, Hannah

Dear Hannah, PHEW!!! I am SO relieved that we are still friends! Hooray! Hooray! Hey! I have an idea. I never used to listen to jazz, but now I kind of like it. And the Jazz Tones are playing a holiday concert in a few weeks. Do you want to come with me? We'll have the best seats in the house. Your friend forever, Abby

Dear Abby, Yippee!!! Of course I want to come with you! That'll be fun. Hey, guess what? Tonight I'm painting a doghouse for a theater set. I can't decide what colors to paint it. What do you think? P.S. Surprise me, okay? Don't say purple!
Your best buddy, Hannah

Dear Hannah, Lime green with orange

trim? Hee-hee-hee. I hope I surprised you.
Purple Hayes

Dear Abby, Orange you glad I asked? (Sorry, that's
BAD.) Ha-ha, Hannah

Ten thousand cheers!

I am so happy. I am also thrilled, excited, relieved, thankful, pleased, giddy, de-
lighted, and overjoyed.
Hannah and I are best friends again!
I didn't tell her about Simon. I wasn't
ready to. But I invited her for a sleepover
this weekend.

Chapter 18

Sunday evening

"Things do not change; we change."

—Henry David Thoreau

That's the Way It Is Calendar

This has been an amazing weekend! On Friday I went to the pizza party at Simon's house. On Saturday, Hannah stayed overnight.

Things That Have Not Changed:
1. Hannah and I are still best friends.
2. I still have a crush on Simon.
3. Simon still barely notices me. (Boo-hoo! But the party was fun. I talked to Einstein and Natalie.)

On Saturday, Hannah had dinner with us, then we watched a movie. We brought our sleeping bags down to the living room and camped out for the night.

After we turned out the lights, we talked for a long time.

Finally, Hannah asked about the Jazz Tones. I could tell she <u>really</u> wanted to know. But I didn't want to tell her.

"You're not going to like it," I said.

"Try me," Hannah said. "I promise I'll listen."

I took a deep breath. "I have a crush on someone," I said.

<u>How We Have Changed:</u>

1. I was scared, but I told Hannah the truth.

2. Hannah didn't get upset. She tried to understand me instead.

I don't know if she really understood. Hannah listened to me as if I were describing a foreign country. I tried to explain what it was like to have a crush, but I couldn't.

Finally, I told her that I needed to get Simon's attention. And that helping out the Jazz Tones was the only way I knew how to do it.

"You'll never get him to notice you by fetching sodas," Hannah said after a moment.

I frowned at her. "What else am I supposed to do?"

"Something that will show him who you really are." Hannah's eyes lit up. "Why don't you write something for the Jazz Tones?"

"Like the words to a song? They have all their music already."

"Don't they put up flyers?" Hannah asked. "Or maybe you can write the program notes."

I practically jumped out of my sleeping bag. "Great idea!"

"If he doesn't know your writing," Hannah pointed out, "he'll never know you."

We spent the next half hour thinking up ways I could use my writing talents for the Jazz Tones.

I can make posters, write ad copy, design and write up programs, and/or submit an article for the school newspaper! Maybe I can interview the saxophone soloist?

Hannah is a genius!

It'll be a lot more fun than writing names on folders. Now Simon will HAVE to notice me.

He will. Now I know how to make it happen.